7/11

The Adventures of the Princess and Mr. Whiffle:

THE THING BENEATH THE BED

The Adventures

of the

Princess and Mr. Whiffle:

THE THING BENEATH THE BED

PATRICK ROTHFUSS

Illustrated by Nate Taylor

SUBTERRANEAN PRESS 2010

Second Printing

ISBN
978-1-59606-131-6

Subterranean Press
PO Box 190106
Burton, MI 48519

www.subterraneanpress.com

Once upon a time, there was a Princess who lived in a marzipan castle.

She lived there all alone.

Except for Mr. Whiffle.
(Who didn't count because he was only a teddy bear.)

And the thing under the bed.

Mr. Whiffle was the Princess' best friend.
They spent all their time together and
had many fabulous adventures.

They found buried treasure by the old stump.

They defeated the Black Duke's rebellion at the battle of Banebridge.

Victory came at a great price. The Princess was sore wounded, and Sir Whiffle was forced to take terrible revenge.

They fought Greenbeard the Pirate...

Though, in the heat of the battle,
Mr. Whiffle was nearly drowned.

And was only saved due to the Princess' quick thinking.

But when her daytime adventures were over,
the Princess always returned to her marzipan castle.

After she had dinner
and washed her face,
she and Mr. Whiffle went to bed.

But they were not alone...

The Princess had never seen the thing under the bed,
because it didn't like the lights.

During the daytime when the bright sun was out
it hid in the deep shadows under the bed.

It even hid at night when the lamps were lit.

That's why the Princess always kept a candle burning.

But some nights,
when it was stormy out,
there were drafts in her room.

And then the Thing didn't need to hide anymore.

The Princess had never seen the Thing,
but she knew what it was like.

It had great wide eyes
that could see in the dark,

and a great, wide mouth
for tasting things.

It had thin, flat lips,

and a wide, flat tongue.

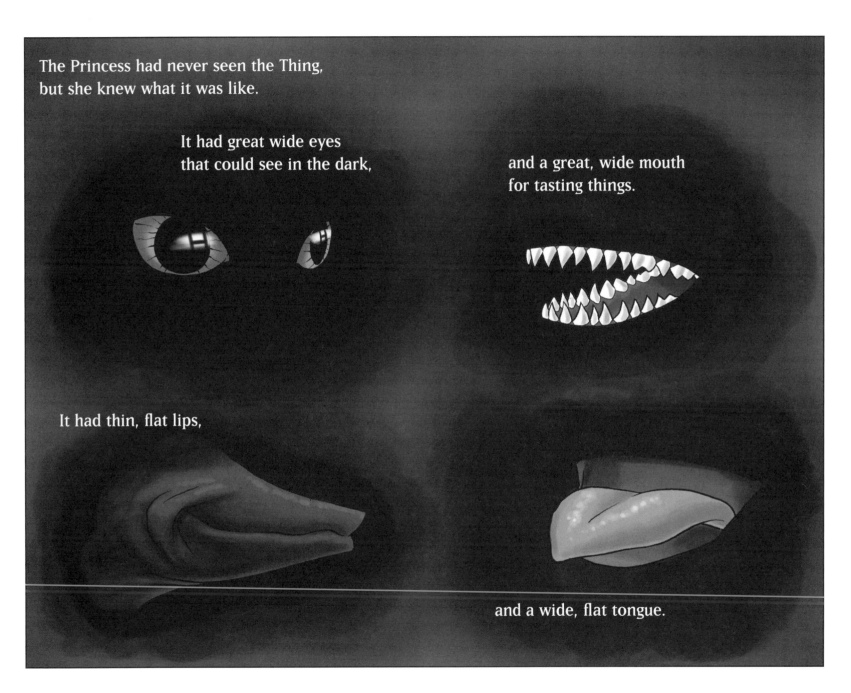

Its skin was greenish-greyish-brownish.

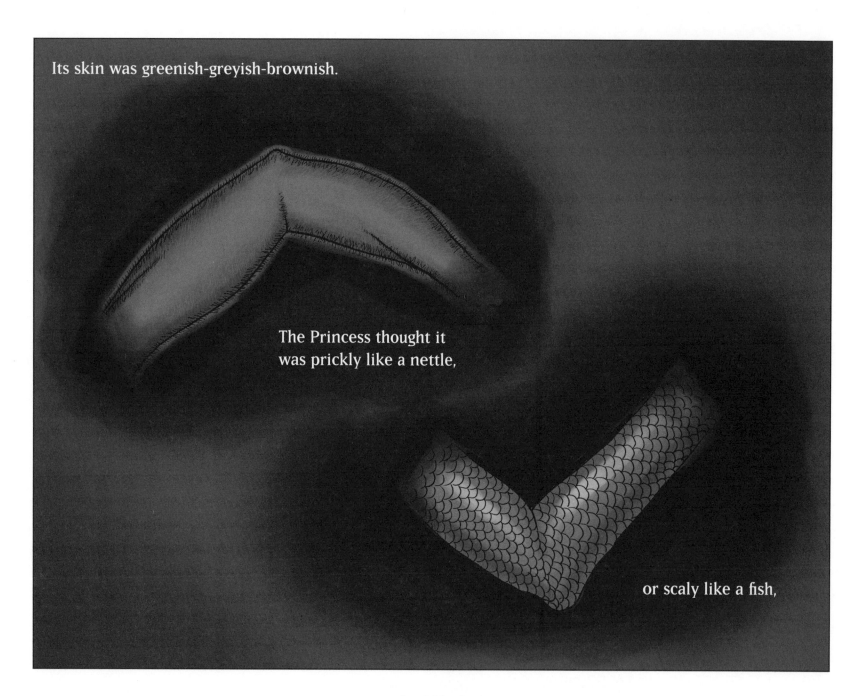

The Princess thought it
was prickly like a nettle,

or scaly like a fish,

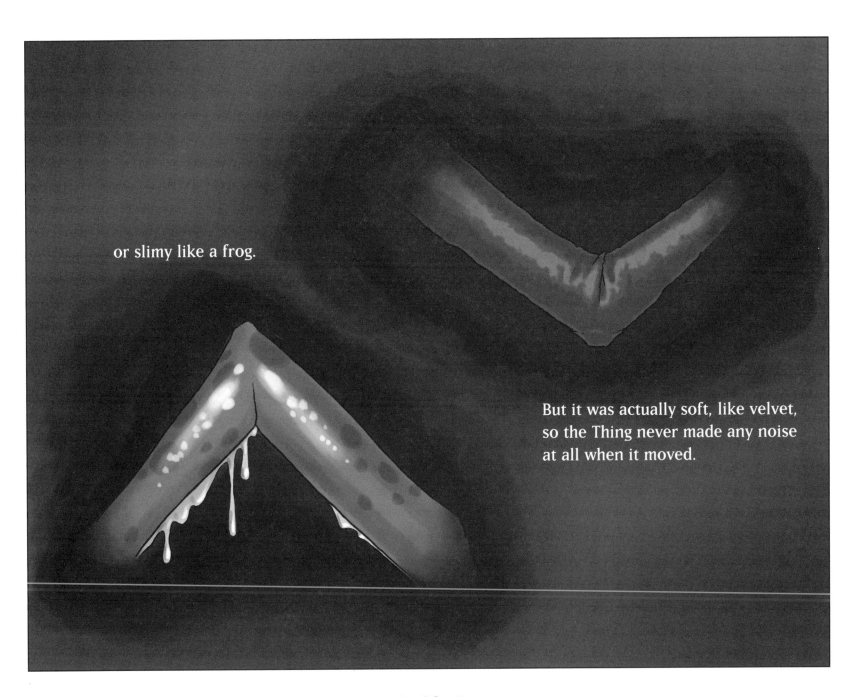

or slimy like a frog.

But it was actually soft, like velvet, so the Thing never made any noise at all when it moved.

The Princess knew it had great big hands,
with great long fingers.

And its long, long arms had an extra elbow.

So it could reach out from under the bed,

...reach up...

Then bend to reach
the top of the bed...

And tickle the Princess silly!

Ending
the First

One day, a package arrived for the Princess.

The Princess loved the kitten.
She and Mr. Whiffle spent a long time
trying to decide what his name should be.

The Princess wanted to call him Mr. Muttonchop because of how he smelled.

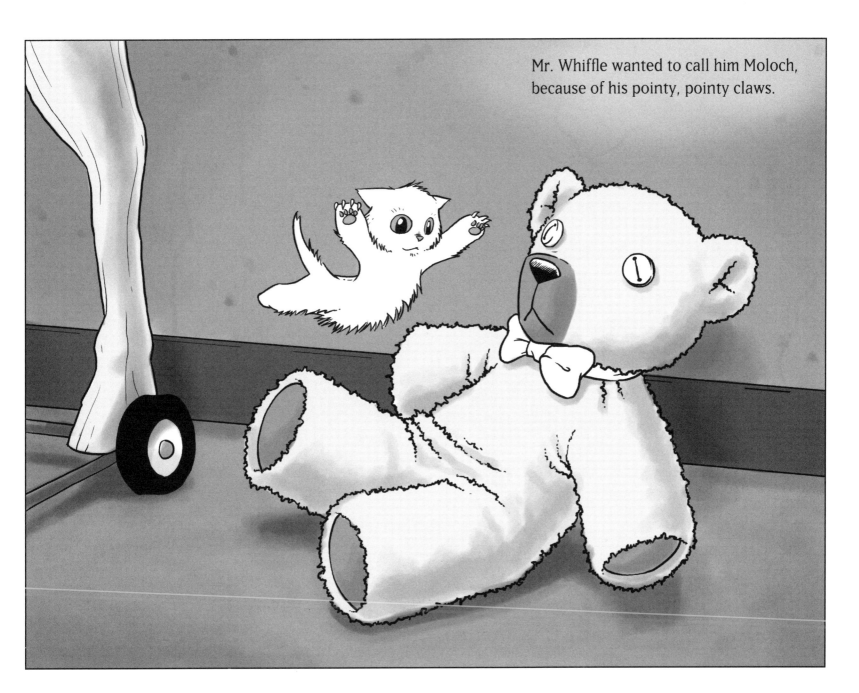

Mr. Whiffle wanted to call him Moloch, because of his pointy, pointy claws.

They compromised by calling him M.M. or 'Emmy' for short.

But then Emmy got lost.

He wasn't in their treasure mine.

Or in the old cave.

Mr. Whiffle suggested they look in the river.
But Emmy wasn't there either.

They knew he couldn't get over the wall.

They looked everywhere.

But they still hadn't found
Emmy by dinnertime.

That night, the Princess couldn't sleep.
Thinking about her lost kitten made her tummy hurt.

Even worse, her candle was short...

And the night was long...

...and her tummy hurt.

Then the Princess heard a noise from under the bed.

She knew it couldn't be the Thing, because it never made any noise except sometimes a soft, velvety rustle.

The noise sounded familiar to the Princess. It was like the sound an animal would make if it wanted to cry out. But it was muffled and quiet.

Then the noise stopped and the Princess heard
a soft velvety sound, like something was
reaching and bending.

Reaching and bending.

Then something wet and warm fell onto her face.

Drip.

Drip.

Drip.

Then mother moon came out from behind a cloud,
and the Princess saw what the Thing was holding.

Ending the Second

It was a big piece
of marzipan!

It was sticky and drippy because the Thing had been eating it.

He wanted to share and be friends.

He was already friends with Emmy.
They had been playing under the bed all day.

Emmy had been trying to call to the Princess, but he couldn't. He'd been eating marzipan with the Thing, and his little kitten mouth was all gummed up. When he tried to mew, it came out *mweh*.

But now they were together again.
And now that the Princess had met the Thing,
she wasn't scared anymore.

And so the Princess ate them.

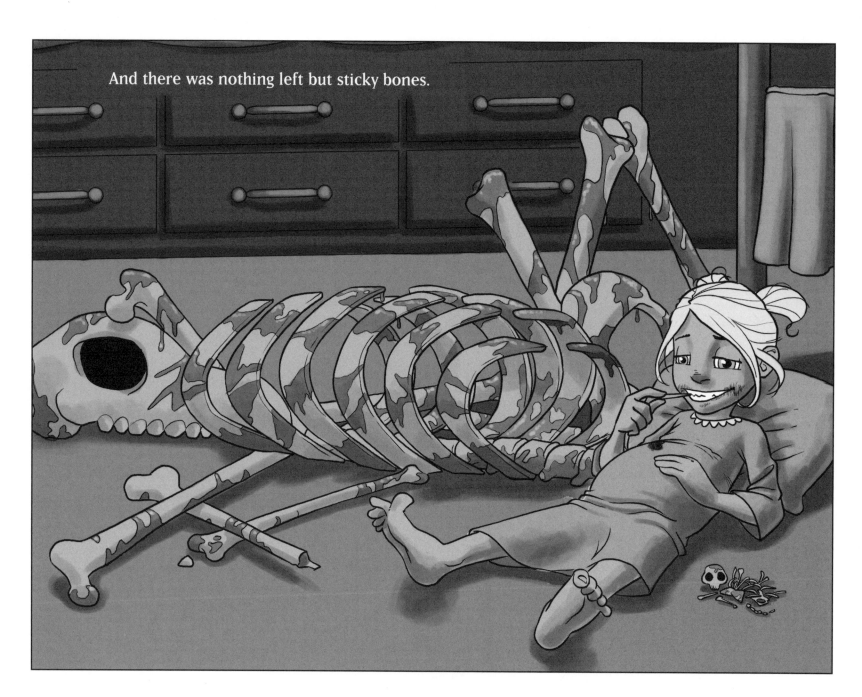

So she and Mr. Whiffle made a fort out of them.

And had tea.

Ending the Third

VSG